D0269404

The
Fish
in
Room
11

*The author would like to acknowledge the support of the Canada Council
for the Arts which last year invested $20.3 million in writing
and publishing throughout Canada.*

*Nous remercions de son soutien le Conseil des Arts du Canada,
qui a investi 20,3 millions de dollars l'an dernier dans les lettres
et l'édition à travers le Canada.*

Canada Council   Conseil des Arts
the Arts   du Canada

Text © Heather Dyer 2004
Illustrations© Peter Bailey 2004

First published in Great Britain in 2004
The Chicken House
2 Palmer Street
Frome, Somerset BA11 1DS
United Kingdom
www.doublecluck.com

Cover design by Ian Butterworth
Cover illustration by Peter Bailey
Designed and typeset by Ian Butterworth
Printed and bound in China

1 3 5 7 9 10 8 6 4 2

British Library Cataloguing in Publication data available.

ISBN 1 904442 33 1

The
Fish
in
Room
11

by Heather Dyer

illustrated by Peter Bailey

The Chicken House

2 Palmer Street, Frome, Somerset BA11 1DS

Chapter 1

Cook's red stockings were the first to escape. They kicked and wriggled on the washing line as though there were legs inside them trying to run away. Then 'twang!' the wind tugged them free of the pegs and they went kicking up into the night sky. Cook's cap was next. Then the tea towels. They snapped and cracked on the line, then one by one they too went flapping off into the dark like a flock of white birds.

No one in the hotel saw them go.

Cook was in the kitchen sucking on the soup spoon – she noticed nothing. Mr Harris was in his office counting out his money – he didn't even look up. In the bar the residents

were busy playing poker – their eyes were on their cards. And Toby (whose fault it all was) was fast asleep in the attic.

Outside the storm raged on. The sign saying 'The Grand' squeaked above the front door of the hotel. The wind brought waves crashing up over the promenade, lifted slates from roofs, sent a broken umbrella cartwheeling down the street, and blew all Cook's laundry out to sea.

Toby woke to the sound of hammering –
BANG-BANG-BANG! 'I know you're up
there!' came a muffled shout.

Hitching up his pyjama bottoms, Toby
clambered out of the pile of old pillows that
he slept in. Then he carefully picked his way
though the battered cardboard boxes, a
dented lampshade and three folded
wheelchairs, to a square in the attic floor. He
lifted the hatch. There at the foot of the
ladder was Cook and she was shaking the
ladder as though it was a tree and she might

shake Toby out of the branches. 'There you are!' she cried. Her hair was wild and her face scarlet.

'What's wrong?' said Toby, alarmed. 'Where's your cap? And your apron?'

'Gone!' cried Cook, slamming her hand on a rung. 'Blown away! Not a *thing* left on the line – and it's Cake Day too!' And with a sob she collapsed on to the ladder with her head on her arms.

Blown away?

All of a sudden Toby remembered the washing that he had pegged out the day before and then forgotten about. 'Oh!' he said softly.

Cook's head flipped up again.

'You better find it,' she told him, 'before Mr Harris finds out. If Mr Harris gets wind of this he'll–'

'Gets wind of what?' came a voice behind her.

Mr Harris had appeared silently, as he often did, surprising people when they least expected it. He was forever listening at doors and spying through keyholes and startling people. He was wearing his maroon dressing gown and matching slippers and his hair was all unkempt and flopping over one eye, making the other eye look even more menacing than usual.

'Well?' he repeated. 'Gets wind of what?'

Cook didn't answer; she was busy tidying her hair and straightening her clothes.

'It's my fault,' said Toby.

'*What is?*' demanded Mr Harris.

'I'll fix it,' said Toby. 'I'm—'

'Fix *what?*' barked Mr Harris, and he put one slipper on to the bottom rung of the ladder and reached up to grab Toby's ankle. Toby jumped back just in time and, leaving Mr Harris cursing below, ran across the attic, opened the skylight and hopped out onto the roof.

He stood there on the slates for a moment, barefoot and in his pyjamas. It was a bright morning and the sea was choppy after the storm. He could see the beach curving away to the opposite headland and all the shops and houses along the seafront with their red brick chimneys and gray slate roofs. But what was that? Something long and red was fluttering from the TV aerial and it looked just like one of Cook's red stockings… It *was* Cook's red stocking! Toby pulled it down and stuffed it into his pyjama pocket. Then he started down the fire escape to find the rest of Cook's lost laundry.

Toby would have loved living in a hotel – had he been allowed to slide down the banisters, sleep in a different bed every night, and hang about in the kitchen waiting to lick out the cake bowl. But of course he wasn't allowed to do any of those things.

Toby had been found in an empty room when he was a baby. One of the chambermaids had discovered him lying on the bed in number 23, wrapped in a blanket with *DD* embroidered on the corner. When she bent over him he had stopped crying, and smiled, and she had picked him up and taken him downstairs.

No one knew where he had come from, and nobody knew who *DD* might be. He was clean (except for a little bit of seaweed between his toes) and he had a tuft of very fine hair on the top of his head. At first, everyone thought someone would come back for him – perhaps he'd been forgotten. So they kept him and waited, but no one came. The staff all took turns at giving him his bottle and so Toby grew up knowing many different faces. They were all young waitresses, different every season.

Mr Harris didn't even know that Toby was there at first, but the boy grew quickly and started running about the red-carpeted corridors, and before long Mr Harris couldn't help noticing the little lad in over-large yellow pyjamas with ships on them.

'Who's that boy in the pyjamas?' he said. 'Hasn't he been here rather a long time?'

When he found out that the boy was not a paying guest ('You mean he's staying here *for free?*') Toby was made to start earning his keep. It was a big old hotel and there was a lot that needed to be done. The Grand stood on the seafront just at the entrance to the pier and although years ago it had been a very grand place, now the paint was peeling on the windowsills and tiles were missing from the roof. Inside, the plush red carpets were wearing thin and the dust lay thick on the skirting boards and picture rails. So as soon as Toby's fingers were strong enough to press down the nozzle on the can of furniture polish he was set about dusting, and as soon as he could be trusted with the china he was given a tea towel and stood on a chair at the draining board.

'I'll keep him on,' said Mr Harris (who would have made him clean the chimneys, too, except that he had heard it wasn't legal). And so Toby remained at The Grand. He worked hard and he played hardly at all, and no one ever thought to buy him clothes or shoes. 'He doesn't need *two* outfits when *one* will do,' said Mr Harris. 'And what does the boy need shoes for? He's not *going* anywhere.' And if Toby was often lonely and often bored he never complained, and so it might have carried on like that forever. But it didn't. Because everything changed the night that Cook's washing blew away.

Chapter 2

Toby stood in front of the hotel. There was a playful wind blowing after the storm and a paper bag and a few chocolate wrappers swirled past like autumn leaves. It was an exciting wind – the sort of wind that seems to have come from a long way away and brings surprises. It was the sort of day, thought Toby, when you might find a shipwrecked sailor lying on the sand, or a message in a green bottle.

The beach was deserted and the pier was closed. The shutters were down on the souvenir kiosks and were rattling in the wind, and the metal claw hung poised over the tank of stuffed toys in the arcade. Apart from an old lady and her small dog on the promenade, Toby was the only one about. But things would soon be different – it was Cake Day. In less than an hour the ship would arrive. Passengers would pour down the gangplank and along the pier and into The Grand for tea and cakes. This reminded Toby that Cook was waiting impatiently for her lost laundry, and he set off in search of it.

Straight away he spotted a wet tea towel clumped on the ground, then he found a tablecloth flapping from the railings and a face cloth in the gutter. He gathered them up and hurried down the ramp to the beach and there he came across Cook's apron, a second tea towel and the other red stocking, all covered with sand. But where was Cook's cap? Toby walked the whole length of the beach and back again but Cook's cap was nowhere to be seen. There was one place however, where Toby still hadn't looked, so he left the bundle of washing on the sand and stepped bravely into the shadows of the pier.

People didn't usually venture under the pier; it was chilly and damp and the water rose and fell restlessly around black, mussel-encrusted pillars. Toby shivered. There was no sign of the cap – just the darkly swilling sea.

But just as he was about to turn back Toby heard a noise – a sharp, cracking noise. Then it stopped.

'Hello?' he called.

There was no reply but the wash of the waves. Toby turned to go but then the noise came again – nearer this time. It sounded just like someone cracking nuts. And what was that? Was something moving out there between the pillars?

'Hello?' called Toby in a shrill voice. 'Who's there?'

For a moment there was no reply, then all of a sudden a girl's pale face peeped out from behind a pillar – and she was wearing Cook's cap! Keeping her eye on Toby, the girl cracked a mussel with her back teeth and ate the meat as though it was a nut.

'Er . . . that's Cook's cap,' said Toby.

'It is?' said the girl.

'Yes.'

The girl tutted. 'All right then,' she said, and the next moment she had left the pillar and was moving swiftly through the water towards Toby. But she was not swimming, she was *gliding* through the water with her arms at her sides and a little wave cresting before her. She came forward almost without effort, as though she was the figurehead of an invisible ship.

Toby took a step backwards.

The girl swept right up to the shore, sending a small wave rushing up on to the sand, and lay there at the water's edge propped up on her elbows with her long green tail swaying gently in the shallows. 'There you are,' she said, and she balled up Cook's cap and tossed it to Toby.

Chapter 3

'I know you,' said the mermaid. 'I've been watching you. We watch everyone – but you're the one we watch the most.'

There was a pause while Toby and the mermaid eyed each other curiously. She was nothing like the mermaids he had seen in picture books. She was so pale that her skin was almost blue, and she looked painfully thin lying there on the sand with the nubs of her shoulder blades sticking out.

'I'm Eliza Flot,' said the mermaid, and put out a hand.

'Toby,' said Toby, taking the thin wet hand and shaking it.

Eliza smiled, and revealed that one of her front teeth was chipped. 'Got any food?' she asked.

Toby hadn't, unfortunately.

'Never mind,' said Eliza, wiping her nose with the back of her hand. 'I'll find something. Chips, maybe.'

'Chips?'

'People throw them to the gulls,' she said. 'They sink.'

'They do?'

'And,' went on Eliza. 'I take the bait off hooks.'

'You eat *worms?*'

'I don't like them much,' she confessed. 'You can feel them trying to get back up.'

Toby swallowed. 'It's Cake Day,' he said. 'If there's anything left I'll bring you some cake.'

Eliza brightened. 'Oh, yes!' she said. But suddenly she broke off, held up her hand for silence, and dunked her head. A moment later she surfaced, blinking the water from her eyes. 'The ship's coming,' she said. 'I can hear it.'

'You can?' Toby peered at the horizon, but there was no sign of the approaching ship, and he couldn't hear anything but the gulls and the wash of the waves.

'Sound travels further underwater,' said Eliza. She was already backing into the sea.

'I'll bring the cake,' said Toby, picking up his bundle of laundry, 'when the ship's gone.'

'You won't tell anyone else, will you?'

'No – promise!'

Halfway up the beach Toby looked back and saw Eliza's small, pale face in the shadows under the pier. He waved. Eliza raised a white arm and dived.

Nigel Harris was standing in the doorway with his arms folded when Toby got back. He was just like his father – thin and sneaky and with a forelock of hair that he was always flicking out of his eyes.

'My dad's been looking for you,' he said.

Toby shouldered his armful of wet washing and made to go past, but Nigel blocked the way.

'Who were you waving at?'

'No one,' said Toby.

'No one?' repeated Nigel. '*Imaginary* friends, is it?'

'No.'

'Who then?'

'Let me past,' said Toby.

'Going to make me?'

Toby peered over Nigel's shoulder. 'No,' he said, 'but Cook will.' And when Nigel turned around to look, Toby slipped past and hurried down the empty corridor. Nigel scowled and looked back towards the beach again. There was *someone* down there, but who?

Chapter 4

The residents were at breakfast. Mr Harris was patrolling the tables with his hands behind his back and the dining room was filled with the murmur of hushed voices and the clink of teacups . . . and there was the Captain at his favourite table. He was wearing his Captain's cap and his Wellington boots and the blazer that he always wore on Cake Days (the navy one with the gold buttons down the front), and his white moustache was curled up elegantly at the corners.

'Aye aye,' he said, waving Toby over. 'Where have you been?'

'Looking for Cook's washing,' Toby told him. 'I forgot about it and it blew away.'

The Captain gave a guffaw, spraying toast crumbs over the tablecloth. 'Ah well,' he said. 'Worse things happen at sea.'

Toby glanced around for Mr Harris but couldn't see him. 'Captain,' said Toby, seizing his chance to talk. 'You've seen a lot of things at sea haven't you?'

'What *haven't* I seen?' boasted the old sailor, spreading more jam on his toast. 'Giant whirlpools, sea cows, white whales . . . '

'But have you ever seen–'

' . . . flying fish and dog fish and lantern fish,' said the Captain, ticking them off on his fingers.

'But what about–'

'Sea serpents and bottle nosed dolphins and–'

'*Mermaids!*' cried Toby, making everyone at the next table look round in surprise. Then, in a lower voice, 'Did you ever see a *mermaid*, Captain?'

The Captain took another big bite of his

toast and jam and chewed thoughtfully before replying. 'No,' he said eventually, 'I can't say I did. I reckon there aren't any left, if there were ever any in the first place. Nobody believes in mermaids now, son.'

'Oh,' said Toby, disappointed. If anyone knew about mermaids it would surely have been the Captain. But before Toby could question him further the Captain held up his finger for quiet and cocked his head. There came the distant bellow of a ship's horn.

'Ship ahoy!' he shouted, banging his fist on the table.

'They're here!' cried someone else.

Then all at once the residents were setting down their teacups and pushing back their chairs.

'All right, all right,' grumbled Mr Harris from the doorway. 'Keep your hair on!' But the residents were already throwing down their napkins and rushing past him. 'I don't see why *everyone* has to go,' said Mr Harris irritably. 'Hey! Wait! Don't forget to *push your chairs in*!'

Toby managed to slip out too, in the crush, and he and the Captain walked right to the very end of the pier to watch the ship come in. What with the wind coming off the sea and the waves heaving and swelling below, Toby could imagine that he was at the prow of an enormous ship. He looked down into the water, half hoping to see Eliza, but there was no one there. The ship was still just a small dark dot in the distance.

The Captain fished a coin out of his blazer pocket. 'Let's look through the telescope,' he said. He put the coin in the slot and Toby angled the telescope towards the horizon. At first all he could see was a sweep of sea and sky, then there it was – a great white ship set in tiers like an enormous wedding cake with rows of little round windows along the sides.

'They're coming!' cried Toby. A moment later the money ran out and everything went black, but the ship was getting nearer all the time and soon it was so close that they could see the passengers on the top deck waving handkerchiefs and streamers. Everyone clapped their hands to their ears as the horn blasted, and the ship pulled up alongside the pier. Then the sailors let down the anchor with a rattling chain and eventually the gangplank was lowered and the passengers poured out. Two by two they descended, like the animals out of the Ark, then down the pier they went, chatting and laughing, and into the hotel for cakes and tea.

In the bustle and the crush no one had noticed the girl peeping out from under the pier – no one but Toby, that is.

'Who are you waving at down there?' asked the Captain.

'No one,' said Toby. And he came away from the railings and headed back down the pier, smiling secretly to himself.

Mr Harris stood by rubbing his hands with glee as the dining room filled up, and Mrs Harris (wearing her best lilac suit and her glasses on a gold chain), was taking people's coats and showing them to their tables. The room rang with chatter and the clink of

cutlery and Toby rushed back and forth cutting cake and bringing out fresh pots of tea. One by one the teapots were emptied, refilled, and emptied again and the cakes disappeared.

'Cakes are going fast today,' remarked Cook, as Toby came staggering into the kitchen under another stack of empty plates.

The pile of profiteroles diminished until there was just a puddle of chocolate sauce left on the plate. The great lemon meringue was sliced smaller and smaller. The mousse was all dished out and the custard squares and the chocolate eclairs disappeared one by one. Toby began to despair that there would be any cakes left at all, when at last the ship's horn sounded to signal its departure.

As one, the passengers put down their teacups, pressed their napkins to their mouths, and scraped back their chairs.

'I don't see why *everyone* has to go and wave goodbye,' said Mr Harris, as the residents filed out after them. And before long all that remained were crumbs on the carpet, sticky knives and a pile of dirty dishes to show that anyone had been there at all...

Toby found Nigel sitting on a chair with his feet up on the kitchen table, eating a custard square.

'Are there any cakes left?' asked Toby.

'Thith wath the latht one,' said Nigel with his mouth full.

No cakes left!

'Here you are,' said Cook. 'You can take these out to the rubbish.' And she shoved a bag into Toby's arms and hustled him out of the back door.

Several seagulls rose from the bins, squawking, as Toby came out. He was just about to heave the bag on to the top of the pile of rubbish when something made him stop and look inside. Cinnamon buns! A whole bag full – just a little bit blackened on the bottom. With a backward glance, Toby clutched the bag of buns to his chest, tiptoed across the yard and slipped out through the back gate.

But no sooner had the seagulls returned to the rubbish than they rose again, screaming, as Nigel opened the back door and, licking his custardy fingers, hurried across the yard after Toby.

Chapter 5

'**E**liza?' called Toby in a low voice. 'Eliza!'

There was a splash, and Eliza slid out from behind one of the pilings.

'Are you alone?' she said.

'Yes,' said Toby. 'I've brought some cakes.' He held up the bag.

Eliza glanced around, then swam quickly to the shore.

'Nobody saw you come?'

'No.'

'Right then,' said Eliza. 'Follow me.' And

she came out of the water and went flopping up the sand on her belly, like a seal.

Toby looked about anxiously. There were a few strollers up on the promenade, and a boy walking his dog further down the beach, but no one seemed to be looking their way. Then there came a wandering cry: 'To-by!'

Nigel! A moment later they heard his footsteps on the boards above. 'To-by!'

'Quick!' hissed Eliza. She was kneeling at the rocky buttress and parting a curtain of seaweed to reveal a dark cleft in the rock. Toby hurried to the crack and stepped through, then Eliza came in after him and the curtain of seaweed swung closed behind them. Inside it was pitch black and it smelled like fish.

'Eliza?'

'Shhh.'

There was the sound of flint striking and light flared up and Toby saw that Eliza was holding a small lantern made out of a sea urchin's shell. She handed it to Toby and shuffled further in. 'This way,' she said.

As they went further down the passage the sounds of the sea disappeared and the tunnel grew silent save for the crackle of Toby's carrier bag and the shuffling of Eliza up ahead. The fishy smell grew stronger. 'Almost there,' called Eliza.

A moment later Toby turned the corner and found himself in an open space – a dim cavern. He held up the lantern and let the light shine round.

The walls were covered with dripping green slime, and on every ledge large enough to hold them were treasures: shells, broken teacups, vases covered in barnacles, old dolls with missing eyes and greening hair, a rusty crown . . . On the ground was a huge pile of broken shells and fish bones gleaming white in the light from Toby's lantern, and at the far side of the cave Eliza was sitting on a barrel, waiting for him. Beside her, a large mermaid that Toby guessed was Eliza's mother was reclining against an orange fishing buoy. The merman lying in a hammock made out of an old fishing net must be her father.

'Come in, come in!' cried Eliza's mother. 'We're so glad you came. Well – look at you! Look at him, Albert! Look how he's grown.' She held out her hand. 'I'm Gaynor.'

Gaynor reminded Toby of a walrus. He stepped forward and shook her hand. It was cold and clammy and covered in rings. Now that he was closer, Toby could see that Gaynor's hair was wet and stringy as though she had just been swimming and let it dry without combing it. There was a smear of mud on her cheek.

'And this,' said Gaynor, 'is Albert.'

Albert put a hand out of the damp blanket he was wrapped in. Toby went over and took it. 'How do you do?' he said politely.

'I – cugh – I – cugh cugh! CAH!' began Albert. 'I–'

Then suddenly Albert threw back his head, took a deep breath, and flung himself forward in a dreadful fit of coughing – and all the while he was gripping Toby's hand like a drowning man. At last he stopped,

took a deep breath and said: 'I'm – cugh – very well, thank you.'

'*Well?*' exclaimed Gaynor. 'Does he *sound* like a well man?'

'There's – cugh! – nothing the matter with me,' said Albert.

Gaynor tutted. 'It's a sad day when mermaids can't even lie on the beach and get a bit of sun,' she said. She looked at Albert and shook her head. 'Damp gets on his lungs,' she explained.

'Good hideaway though, eh?' wheezed Albert. 'You'd never have guessed we were here would you?' and he winked at Gaynor. 'No one's found us yet, have they, love?'

'Not yet,' said Gaynor. 'But I live in fear that . . . but lets not talk about it,' she said. 'This is a special occasion!'

'I've got cakes,' said Toby, rummaging in his bag.

Eliza clapped her hands. 'Cakes!' she cried. 'That's what I was telling you about, Mum.'

Toby handed round the cinnamon buns (no one complained about the burnt bits) and Albert flipped out of his hammock and made a little fire and brewed a pot of seaweed tea. Toby was glad of the hot drink, even though it was salty.

'We never used to live like this,' Gaynor told him. And while they ate their cakes and sipped seaweed tea out of cracked china cups, the Flots told Toby how things used to be.

Chapter 6

'**B**ack then, you didn't have to worry,' said Gaynor. 'People thought it was good luck to see a mermaid – now they'd think they were losing their minds.'

'Times change,' said Albert.

'Remember the full moon parties?' said Gaynor.

'And body surfing in the autumn storms!'

'And sunbathing with the seals!'

'We had a good time, didn't we, love?'

'We did,' said Gaynor. 'We worry for Eliza though. We'd like her to get out a bit, see the world, but . . .'

'Don't go on, Mum,' said Eliza, embarrassed.

'It's no place for a growing girl,' said Gaynor, 'stuck indoors with us.'

'All the other mermaids have gone,' said Albert.

'Yes,' said Gaynor. 'They all went off to find somewhere better. Those that stayed all met an unpleasant end. Fishing nets or . . .' Here Gaynor caught her breath and shook her head and Albert put his arm around her shoulders.

'There, there,' he said.

Gaynor pulled herself together and smiled at Toby bravely. 'We needn't dwell on that,' she said. 'Toby's here! Let's talk of nicer things.'

They chatted on in the dark of the cave with the firelight flickering on the walls, and it was difficult to know how much time was passing.

'I ought to go,' Toby said eventually. 'They'll be wondering where I am.'

'The tide!' cried Gaynor, clapping her hand to her mouth. 'I'd completely forgotten.'

'Oh dear,' said Albert.

'The tide is rising,' explained Eliza. 'At high tide the water comes right up the passage.'

'It has its advantages,' said Albert, smiling at Toby's expression. 'No one sees you coming and going when your door is four feet under!'

Toby seized the lantern and stood up.

'Wait a minute,' said Albert. 'Before he goes, give the lad something to take back with him.'

'Of course!' cried Gaynor, and she shuffled forwards a few inches and took a small barnacle-encrusted chest from the top of a pile stacked against the wall. Toby held the lantern near as Gaynor turned a rusty old key in the lock and opened the lid to reveal a tangle of necklaces and gems. She rummaged through the jewellery as though it were a box of old buttons. 'Ouch!' she said, sucking her finger. 'A brooch.' But presently she pulled something out, breathed on it, rubbed it against her bosom, and held it up.

'The sovereign?' said Albert. 'Excellent choice, excellent. How appropriate.'

'It's a small one,' said Gaynor. 'It used to
be a duke's signet ring. We've been keeping
it for just the right person.' And she took
Toby's hand and slipped the ring on to his
middle finger. At first it wouldn't go but she
twisted it firmly over the knuckle. 'There we
are!' she said. 'Splendid.'

'That's a man's ring, that is,' said Albert admiringly, and he winked at Gaynor.

The ring had a flat top with a coin set in it, and something stamped into the gold that Toby couldn't make out in the dim light. It felt rather heavy on his hand, and his fingers wouldn't fit together properly with it on.

Eliza giggled. 'Come on,' she said. 'We'd better go.'

'Good to – cugh! – meet you, son,' said Albert.

Gaynor yanked Toby forward into a hug. 'Come again soon,' she said.

Eliza shuffled back down the tunnel and Toby followed with the lantern, plunging Albert and Gaynor into darkness behind him. Even after they had made several turns Toby could still hear the diminishing echoes of Albert coughing, coughing, coughing fit to crack. The floor of the tunnel was now swilling with water and the further they went the deeper it got until Toby had to stop and roll up his pyjama bottoms. It was cold and

42

black and pulled at his ankles.

But presently there came a new sound – a distant roar – and Toby saw a chink of light at the end of the tunnel. Eliza stopped and took the lantern. 'Hurry,' she said.

Toby slipped through the seaweed curtain and out into the daylight. The fresh air was a relief after the stale fishy smell of the cave and Toby hurried back up the beach, hoping that no one had noticed he was gone. He crept up to the front door of the hotel, turned the handle and . . .

'Aha!' shrieked Mr Harris, seizing Toby by the collar. 'Caught in the act!'

Chapter 7

'**I** told you, Dad,' said Nigel.

'Cake stealer!' said Mr Harris, shaking Toby like a rat.

'*And* he ate them all himself,' muttered Nigel. 'Little pig.'

But Toby was choking on the neck of his pyjamas and couldn't reply.

Mr Harris let him go. Toby's hands flew to his neck and then, remembering the ring, he whipped them behind his back again.

'He's got something,' observed Nigel.

'It's nothing,' said Toby, twisting desperately at the gold ring.

Mr Harris held out his hand. 'Let's have it,' he said.

'I can't,' said Toby.

'*Can't?*' roared Mr Harris.

'I can't get it *off*,' said Toby, and, miserably he brought round his hand and showed them the ring. Mr Harris yanked at it.

'Ow!' cried Toby.

Seizing Toby's finger, Mr Harris dragged him into the bar to examine the ring under the lamp. There was a pause while he turned the ring – and Toby's finger – this way and that under the light.

'Interesting,' he said eventually, '*very* interesting. People have been looking for this ring for a *very long time.* WHERE DID YOU GET IT?'

Toby just pressed his lips together and said nothing.

Mr Harris twisted Toby's finger spitefully, and glared at him. '*Where did you get it?*' he repeated.

'Ouch!' Toby yelped. 'You're hurting!'

'He must have found it,' said Nigel.

'Did you?' snapped Mr Harris.

'I . . . I . . . I can't tell you,' stuttered Toby.

'Can't tell me? Then you'll show me!' and holding Toby by the collar, Mr Harris marched him back outside and down the ramp on to the beach.

'Ugh!' said Mr Harris distastefully. 'My slippers.'

'That's where he went,' said Nigel, pointing. 'He must have found it under there,' and they picked their way across the sand and peered at the black water swilling beneath the pier.

'It's creepy, Dad,' said Nigel.

'Shut up,' said Mr Harris.

They were only steps from the Flots' cave, and Toby was grateful that the rising tide had covered the sand and hidden his footsteps to the cave entrance. He tried not to look in that direction and give it away.

'Here? Was it here?' Mr Harris asked, hauling Toby after him. 'There? What about there?'

'Maybe,' stammered Toby. 'Maybe not.'

'I bet he's got a stash,' said Nigel.

'Well?' said Mr Harris, shaking Toby again. 'Are there any more?'

'What – rings?'

'What else?'

'I didn't *see* any,' Toby said truthfully.

But Mr Harris would not believe him. 'We'll find the rest,' he said. 'It's just a matter of time.' And he staggered about in the muck until eventually he took an unfortunate turn and landed squarely on his backside. Toby helped him up again and, cursing, Mr Harris marched him back to the hotel.

Mrs Harris came out from the office just as they walked in. 'Kenneth!' she exclaimed, peering at the mud on the seat of her husband's trousers. 'Where have you *been?*' But Mr Harris ignored his wife and dragged Toby, by his ring finger, into the kitchen.

He tried everything he could think of to remove that ring. He twisted it. He turned it. He put it on ice. He clamped it with the tongs, and tugged. But nothing worked, and

Toby's finger grew red and swollen like a sausage.

'It won't come off!' cried Mrs Harris, wringing her hands in distress. 'We'll have to get the doctor.'

'Doctor? We don't need a *doctor*,' said Mr Harris, seizing the cleaver. 'I'll do the honours.'

'No!' sobbed Toby.

'No!' cried Cook and Mrs Harris, covering their eyes.

'*Dad*!' gasped Nigel.

'Perhaps you're right,' said Mr Harris, reconsidering. 'We might damage it.'

'The finger?'

'No, the ring.'

'It just wants a little lubrication,' said Cook.

So they greased Toby's finger with olive oil, they lathered it in soap, they buttered it up. Everyone had a go. Mr Harris grew angrier and angrier, until his face throbbed scarlet, just like Toby's poor finger.

'Stop it, Kenneth!' said Mrs Harris eventually. 'Enough is enough! You're hurting him.'

'She's right,' said Cook. 'We'll pull his

finger off.'

Mr Harris tutted in exasperation. 'All *right*,' he said, flinging Toby's hand away. 'You can keep it for now. Go and clean the bins or something!' And he swept out of the kitchen. Nigel hesitated, then hurried after him.

He caught up with his father in the bar. 'You're going to let him *keep* it?' he asked.

'Yes, Nigel, I'm going to let him *keep* it,' mimicked Mr Harris. He took another swig of brandy. 'You see, if you'd looked a little more *closely*,' he continued, 'you might have noticed whose *head* was on that ring. Yes! And if you'd been using your *brain* for a change, you might have realized (like I did) that there's a lot more to gain here than just a ring.'

Nigel tried to look as though he understood what his father was talking about.

'Oh yes,' went on Mr Harris. 'It could really *put us on the map*, this ring. It could make us a tourist attraction! But listen . . .' And here he glanced round to make sure that no one was listening. 'I want you to keep an eye on that boy,' he said. 'Don't let him out of your sight. Got it?'

'Yes, Dad,' said Nigel.

That night Toby sat under the attic skylight for a long time, examining the ring by the light of the moon. He could make out the head of a man wearing a large hat. Beneath the head were the words *Duke of Dudley,* and a date that he couldn't quite decipher. Hadn't Cook told him a duke had been shipwrecked off this beach ten years ago? Could it be *this* duke? The Duke of Dudley?

If only Mr Harris hadn't seen the ring!

Toby thought of the Flots in their dark hideaway beneath the pier. Mr Harris wouldn't rest until he had combed the whole beach for more valuables – and what if he found the cave? Toby twisted the ring hopelessly on his shiny, swollen finger, and a tear rolled down his cheek. He had only just made friends with the Flots, and already he had put them in danger. He would have to help them. He would have to warn them, somehow. But how?

Chapter 8

Up in room 22, Margot was dreaming. In her dream Margot was a girl again, back in the good old days when her father had managed The Grand Hotel. Margot's sisters were in the dream as well. 'Catch me if you can!' shrieked Louise, running down the beach in her long white skirts, and Margot and the others all ran after her, laughing and holding on to their hats so that the wind wouldn't carry them off.

Those were the days! Times had been happier then. When Margot's father had managed The Grand the hotel had been filled with chatter and laughter and there were cakes *every* day, not just on Cake Day. There was always a brass band playing on the promenade, and people danced in the evenings. Margot and her sisters had been allowed to stay up late and slide down the banisters and do all the sort of things that Toby wasn't.

But then everything had changed. Margot's father died. Margot took it ever so hard, everyone said. Then one by one, in the space of a year, all her sisters had married and moved away. Margot spent more and more time in her room, and her cousin Kenneth Harris started running the hotel. Eventually the music stopped. The laughter died.

Nowadays Margot rarely left her room at all, preferring instead to take her meals on a tray and spend the day looking through her photograph albums, living in her memories while life went on outside. Her visits from Toby were the only thing she really looked forward to.

Margot was awoken by a knock at the

door. She opened her eyes. The room was still, the curtains drawn, a cup of cold tea was standing on the bedside table. But what was all that commotion down on the beach?

'Come in!' she called, propping herself up with pillows.

In came Toby bearing a breakfast tray with a boiled egg, a teapot and the newspaper. 'Morning,' he said. He put the tray on the bedside table and kissed Margot's cheek. Then he went to open the curtains and stood at the window for a moment, looking down. The beach was a changed place. It was crawling with activity. Several people were digging with garden spades and plastic shovels, and others were buzzing over the sands with what looked like metal detectors.

'What's going on down there?' asked Margot, pouring herself a cup of tea.

'They're looking for treasure.'

'Treasure?'

Toby came away from the window and handed Margot the newspaper. She reached for her reading glasses and balanced them over her nose with one finger while she read.

'LOCAL BOY FINDS DUKE'S RING,' proclaimed the headlines. There was a picture of Toby wearing a startled expression and Mr Harris standing behind him beaming widely with his hand clamped on Toby's shoulder. Beneath the picture the caption read:

'Toby, odd job boy at The Grand, has found a signet ring believed to have belonged to the late Duke of Dudley.'

Margot glanced at Toby over her glasses. Then she read on:

'Mr Kenneth Harris told the *Weekly News* yesterday that the ring was found on the beach outside his hotel. Dr Seaworthy, director of ocean sciences at Bodlum University, speculates that the duke's jewels must have been disturbed by recent storms, and washed ashore.'

'Washed ashore?' said Margot. 'Who ever heard of jewels being washed ashore?' She folded the paper thoughtfully. 'Could I see that ring?'

It had been a whole day before the swelling had gone down and Toby had managed to slip the ring off his finger. He took it from his pyjama pocket and put it in Margot's palm. She turned the ring this way and that under the bedside light, and eventually she handed it back to Toby and took off her glasses. 'Remarkable,' she said. 'Fancy that! Nobody thought those jewels would ever turn up again. It's almost as if–'

'What jewels?'

'Well,' said Margot, 'ten years ago a duke's ship went down not far from here. He was on his way back from America with the family jewels – they'd been on display in a museum there. It was very sad. He had his wife and his only son with him, too – the boy was just a baby. Nearly everyone on the ship drowned, and they never did find the body of the baby boy. A few sailors made it to shore, though, and they always said that the reason they survived was because they were rescued.'

'Rescued?'

'Rescued by *mermaids*,' said Margot. 'And when the divers went to salvage the wreckage, they found nothing – nothing but empty lockers. All the jewels had gone. The locals searched the shores for weeks. The duke had no surviving relatives you see, so it was finders keepers – but nothing was ever found. Nobody could explain it. The sailors said the mermaids must have taken the treasure, but of course nobody believed them. You know what sailors are like, full of tall tales. Anyway, mermaids haven't been seen here since . . . Well, for a very long time.'

There was a pause.

'Margot,' Toby said carefully. 'Do *you* believe in mermaids?'

Margot was quiet for a moment. She picked up a photograph from the bedside table and regarded it thoughtfully. It was a picture of herself as a young girl wearing a bonnet and a long dress, paddling in the sea. She put the photograph back on the table with a sigh.

'Things were different then,' she said. 'This

was a happy house. There used to be singing after supper and a band on the promenade. And on a full moon people used to say that you could hear the mermaids singing . . .'

'So there *were* mermaids?' interrupted Toby.

Margot hesitated. 'Well,' she said, 'I was only a girl then, but one day I saw something I've never forgotten. You know the place – just beyond the pier where the rocks come down to the water?'

'Yes.'

'I heard singing. It was a girl's voice – very lovely. When I turned the corner I saw that there was someone sitting on a rock, a little way off shore. It was early and the sun was just coming up. She was singing to the sunrise.'

Here Margo took a sip of her tea, and Toby waited.

'The song ended,' said Margo, 'and I started clapping. As soon as she heard me, she looked around, startled. But when she saw it was only a girl she smiled and gave a little wave. I waved back, and then she slipped into the water head first – smooth, like a seal. Then she was gone.'

'Did you ever see her again?' asked Toby.

'No,' said Margot, 'I never did. But sometimes, on a summer evening, with my window open, I could hear her singing.'

Then Margot seemed to rouse herself. 'So, where *did* you get the ring?' she asked.

Toby hesitated for just a moment. 'I was given it,' he said, 'by mermaids.'

Margot's teacup clattered into her saucer and she looked at Toby for a long time, then she turned her eyes to the window where the sounds of the treasure seekers rose from below.

'They're still here?'

'Yes,' said Toby. 'Under the pier.'

Chapter 9

Margot sat motionless as Toby explained. He told her how he had first met Eliza, and how she had taken him back to their damp cave that filled with seawater twice a day. He told her about the ring, and how Mr Harris had told the newspapers and the television people about it, and that people from far and wide had come to the beach to find the rest of the treasure.

Margot sighed. 'Mr Harris always was a greedy child,' she told Toby. 'Even when he was a boy it was always: "Kenneth Harris!

Put it back you've had enough", or "Kenneth! Let your sister have a turn". He always thought that people would *take advantage* – goodness knows why. He used to keep his books locked up so that no one else could borrow them. And the lies he told!' She shook her head sadly. 'I had no idea that things had got so out of hand. And twisting your finger like that! I should have seen this coming.' Margot took Toby's hands in hers and pressed them tightly. 'I'm so sorry,' she said. 'I should have taken care of things – and you – long before it got to this.'

Toby cast his eyes down. 'Never mind about me,' he said. 'It's the Flots who need help now. What if someone finds that secret passage and—'

'Stop!' said Margot. 'I can't bear to think about it. Can't they go elsewhere?'

'They've nowhere else to go.'

They thought about this for a minute, and then Toby looked up and said: 'Unless they come here.'

'Here?' said Margot. 'To the hotel?'

'We could disguise them,' said Toby.

'Disguise them as what?'

'I don't know,' admitted Toby.

'Never mind,' said Margot briskly. 'We'll think of something. But first things first. I've been in bed for far too long and I've been shirking my responsibilities. It's time I got up.' And she flung back the covers and threw her legs over the edge of the bed.

Toby passed Margot her quilted dressing gown.

'I know!' she said, struggling to get her arm into a sleeve. 'Why don't they come as ladies riding sidesaddle?'

'People don't do that any more,' said Toby, 'unless it's a parade'.

'What about those litters with curtains that pull across?'

'I think it might attract a crowd,' said Toby, passing Margot her walking stick.

'Stretchers, then! We could pretend that they've just come from the hospital.'

'But who would carry them?'

Margot took a first, shaky step forwards.

'My! It's been longer than I thought,' she gasped, and leaning heavily on Toby's shoulder she made her way towards the door.

'Are you sure you wouldn't like a wheelchair?' asked Toby as they staggered out into the hall. 'There's three of them in the attic with . . .' Suddenly he stopped. '*Wheelchairs*,' he said.

Margot stared at him. 'Of course!'

'But how do we get a message to the Flots?' said Toby. 'The beach is crowded day and night and if anyone saw me sneaking to the cave . . .'

'Out of the question,' said Margot firmly. 'We'll have to think of another way.'

'Yes,' said Toby thoughtfully. 'Another way . . .' They stood there for a moment, then Toby said: 'I could do it if I had a boat.'

'A boat?'

'And a pipe.'

'A pipe?'

'And I'll need some help,' said Toby. 'Someone who knows about boats, someone

Tired of digging?

Teas at The GRAND

who's had a lot of experience at sea . . .'

'Oh dear,' said Margot. 'I don't know anyone like that.'

'I do,' said Toby suddenly. 'I know just the person!'

But there was no opportunity to carry out his plan that day or the next since the beach was crawling with treasure seekers and Toby was made to walk up and down in front of the hotel wearing a signboard bearing a picture of a chocolate éclair and the words:

'TIRED OF DIGGING? TEAS AT THE GRAND.'

'Cheer up, Toby!' said Mr Harris spitefully, jingling pockets full of change. 'This is where the real treasure is!' Mr Harris had erected a makeshift stall at the head of the pier and was making a quick profit in plastic buckets and spades. 'This could be your lucky day,' he told an old lady as she hobbled off towards the beach. 'Put your back into it!'

Toby watched the scene from under his signboard. The beach was pocked with holes. There were men in suits skimming the sand with metal detectors, dogs and children digging on all fours – even a group of Girl Guides conferring round a map. And further up the beach there was a small bulldozer gouging out a great pit with its metal claw. So far nothing had been found. But how long would it be before someone discovered the cave?

Toby jumped when he realized that someone was speaking to him. It was Nigel. He was leaning in the doorway of The Grand and had just taken a green lollipop out of his mouth. 'They'll find them eventually, of course,' he was saying. 'It's only a matter of time.'

'What?' said Toby.

'I said they'll find them eventually,' repeated Nigel. 'You can't keep them a secret forever.'

'Keep who a secret?' said Toby in alarm.

'The *jewels*,' Nigel said. Then he looked at Toby sharply. 'What else?'

'Nothing!' said Toby, and he turned quickly and walked the other way.

Nigel watched him go. Then he put the lollipop back in his mouth and sucked on it thoughtfully.

Chapter 10

The following day everything changed. It rained. The treasure hunters had packed up and driven away or had crowded into The Grand for tea and cakes, and the beach was deserted.

Nigel was sulking. He had caught a cold that had turned his eyes pink, and Mr Harris had told him to keep out of the way lest he put the guests off their cake. Now Nigel was sitting up in his room watching television with a pile of tissues festering beside the bed.

All of a sudden he heard the front door shut with a bang. He got up, went to the window, and parted the curtains. Who could be going out on a day like today?

Two bulky figures in hooded yellow
raincoats were going down the ramp to the
beach. A man and a boy. They must be
pretty desperate, thought Nigel, to be digging
in this weather. But wait a minute! That boy
had no shoes on. It could only be Toby –
Toby and the Captain. And what were they
carrying? It didn't look like buckets and
spades – more like a picnic hamper and two
oars and . . . a length of pipe? Nigel frowned.
They were always plotting, those two. Did
the Captain think he was Toby's *dad* or
something? Well, whatever they were up to
they weren't going to get away with it. Nigel
left the window and hurried downstairs to
find his jacket and boots.

'Here she is!' said the Captain proudly. 'Just
like you wanted.' And he pulled away the
blue tarp with a flourish, revealing a boat
upturned on the sand. It was a metal boat,
scratched and dented, with green weeds and
barnacles growing along the keel. 'Isn't she a
beauty?'

Toby's face fell. 'Are you sure it floats?' he said.

'Of course she floats,' said the Captain, looking hurt.

Together they dragged the boat down to the water and climbed in. The Captain staggered to the far end, sat down abruptly, and put on his peaked cap. Then he picked up the oars and began to row with gusto,

sending water flying into the boat at each stroke.

'They don't call me the Captain for nothing,' he said.

Toby bailed out the water with a plastic cup as the Captain rowed further and further out until the shore was just a dark line behind them.

'I think this might be far enough,' said Toby.

The Captain dropped the oars with a clatter. 'Whew!' he gasped. 'I'm a little out of practice.'

The rain was coming down hard now and the dirty water that had collected in the bottom of the boat swilled back and forth with the motion of the waves. It was choppy out here and it seemed that the shore was a long way away.

'Right, then,' said the Captain. 'No one can overhear us now. Can't you tell me what's going on?'

'Well,' said Toby, 'I came out here to contact some . . . friends.'

'Ah!' said the Captain. 'Why didn't you say so!' And he rustled inside his jacket and produced a pair of binoculars.

'Are you sure we're on time?' he said, scanning the horizon. 'I can't see a vessel.'

'They're not coming by boat,' said Toby.

'Not coming by boat?' exclaimed the Captain. 'What then – submarine?' He laughed.

Toby shook his head.

'Plane?'

Toby shook his head again. 'They'll be swimming,' he said.

There was a pause. *'Swimming?'* said the Captain.

Back at The Grand, Nigel was rummaging in the cupboard under the stairs, tossing shoes and woolly hats out into the hall.

'Nigel!' exclaimed Mrs Harris, coming to see what all the clatter was about. 'What are you looking for?'

'Boots,' came Nigel's muffled voice from the depths of the cupboard as a snowshoe flew out and hit the opposite wall.

'You're going out on a day like today?'

Nigel emerged from the cupboard with cobwebs in his hair. 'Where have you put them?' he demanded.

'I haven't put them anywhere,' said Mrs Harris. 'They're right where you left them. At the front door.'

Nigel made an exasperated noise and stomped down the hall. Sure enough, there

were his boots standing below the coat rack.
He stuffed his feet into them.

'Where are you going?' asked his mother.
But Nigel had already shrugged on his coat
and gone out, slamming the door behind
him. Mrs Harris sighed and started to put
everything back in the cupboard.

Chapter 11

Toby took up the pipe and lowered one end into the water.

'What are you doing?' cried the Captain, gripping the gunnels with white knuckles. 'You're rocking the boat!'

Toby put his mouth to the end of the pipe. 'Testing,' he said. 'Testing. One, two. One, two.' His words echoed down the tube and were swallowed by the sea. 'Calling the Flots! Toby to Flots! Calling the Flots to the silver boat east of the pier!' Then he pulled the pipe up out of the water again, and put it in the bottom of the boat. 'Sound travels further,' he said, 'underwater.'

The Captain was staring at Toby in amazement. 'But who will hear it?' he said.

If Nigel squinted through the rain he could just make out the boat with two figures sitting at either end, but couldn't quite see what they were doing. Then he remembered the telescope. Feeling in his pockets for loose change, he ran to the end of the pier, slotted a coin into the telescope and put his eye to the end.

At first Nigel wasn't able to distinguish the sky from the sea. Everything was grey. Then all of a sudden the little boat swung into view and there were Toby and the Captain in their waterproof coats.

The Captain was looking rather pale, and concentrating on taking big deep breaths to stop himself being sick. Toby, meanwhile, was tapping the metal hull with a teaspoon, the sound ringing out loudly through the rain. Every so often he would pause and turn this way and that, scanning the horizon.

'I don't feel well,' said the Captain weakly. 'And I don't think your friends are coming. Let's go back.'

'Wait,' Toby begged. 'I *know* they'll come. Just wait a minute.'

But the Captain had already taken up the oars and was beginning to row slowly back to shore. 'I don't know who you're signalling,' he gasped. 'But in my day we didn't use pipes and tea—'

He stopped suddenly. From just behind him there came a wet explosion like a whale blowing.

'Albert!' said Toby with relief. 'I thought you'd never come.'

Startled, Nigel knocked his eyebrow painfully on the end of the telescope. What was that? Something round like a head had popped up right beside the boat. Surely there couldn't be someone swimming way out there? He tried to focus in more closely but all of a sudden everything went black. His money had run out! He thumped the telescope in frustration but only managed to hurt his hand. He cursed and hurried back through the rain.

Albert swam to the side of the boat. 'Pleasure to meet you,' he said to the Captain, reaching up. Dumbstruck, the Captain leaned out and put his hand in Albert's, but instead of shaking it, Albert gripped the hand tightly and used it to haul himself aboard. The Captain leaped out of the way as Albert fell flapping into the bottom of the boat.

'Don't worry! No need to panic!' Albert reassured him, lifting himself on to a seat. 'I'm quite all right!'

The Captain did not reply; he was staring open mouthed at Albert's blue-green tail.

'What a day!' said Albert, wringing out his beard.

Just then there was another geyser as Eliza surfaced. 'Eliza!' cried Toby, reaching out to help her in, but Eliza waved his hand away and struggled up on to the gunnels with her elbows akimbo. Eventually she toppled head first into the grey water sluicing about in the bottom of the boat. 'Ugh!' she said, wiping her mouth with the back of her hand.

'And here's Gaynor!' announced Albert.

By now, the Captain had recovered sufficiently to remember his manners. Together, he and Albert leaned out to help Gaynor into the boat.

'Thank you, gentlemen,' she said, offering them each a jewelled hand. But out of the water Gaynor was a heavy load. It took them both to haul her aboard and the boat keeled dangerously – even with Toby and Eliza leaning to the other side to balance it.

Eventually they were all seated.

'I think we could all do with a cuppa,' said the Captain weakly.

He passed round a thermos of hot sweet tea and shared out cheese and tomato sandwiches and shortcake biscuits. The Flots ate hungrily, slurping hot tea while the rain plinked down. They ate all the sandwiches and the shortcake biscuits and drank most of the tea, and when they had finished Eliza asked if there was any more. There wasn't.

'So,' said Albert. 'What's going on at the beach?'

Toby sighed. 'It's all my fault,' he said. 'It

was the ring – Mr Harris saw it and he told the newspapers and now everyone's searching for the rest of the treasure. That's why I called you here. You can't stay in the cave now. It's far too dangerous.'

'But we've nowhere else to go,' said Gaynor in distress. 'What can we do?'

'You can stay at the hotel.'

'*Your* hotel?'

'Yes.'

'The Grand!' cried Eliza, clapping her hands. 'We're going to stay at The Grand!' and she grabbed Toby and jigged up and down in excitement.

'Just a minute,' said the Captain, steadying himself, for Eliza was making the boat rock dangerously. 'Have you asked Mr Harris about this?'

'He'll never know,' said Toby.

'Never know? But how—'

'They'll be disguised.'

'Disguised?' cried Eliza. 'Oh, goody!' Then she paused. 'Disguised as what?'

Toby glanced around as though to check

that no one could overhear. 'We'll have to be careful,' he said, 'but I think it will work. Here's the plan . . .'

Chapter 12

'**B**rrrring brrrrriiiiing!' Mr Harris dreamed he could hear the phone ringing and turned in his sleep. There was never a moment's rest! He pulled the covers up over his head to shut out the sound. But the ringing was going on and on. Why didn't someone answer that? He reached out groggily and grabbed the telephone.

'Hello?' he mumbled.

'Brrrrrining!' went the doorbell again, followed by the sound of someone hammering on the front door.

Mr Harris slammed down the phone and got out of bed. He threw on his maroon dressing gown and stepped into his slippers.

'Who could that be?' said Mrs Harris. 'It's six o'clock in the morning!'

'I'm about to find out!' snapped Mr Harris, flinging open the bedroom door and marching down the hall.

All along the corridor residents' heads were looking out of their rooms, but they ducked back in again as Mr Harris swept past with his dressing gown flapping out behind him. Other residents were huddled at the top of the stairs in their pyjamas and nightdresses, squinting down to try and make out who was beyond the frosted glass of the front door.

'Morning, Mr Harris!' said the Captain. But Mr Harris did not reply. The residents parted to let him through and he stomped down the stairs and flung open the door. Abruptly the ringing stopped – but before Mr Harris could say a word the Flots had wheeled in across the threshold, bringing with them the salty smell of the sea.

'Yoo-hoo!' cried Gaynor, waving up at the residents.

The residents waved back uncertainly. From the top of the stairs they stared down at the three curious figures in wheelchairs. The first was a very large woman in a purple hat. She wore a matching purple dress that came right down to the footrest with just the tips of her glittery shoes poking out from beneath the hem. The hand that the woman waved was covered in rings and her throat was heavy with necklaces, which glittered under the hall light. Behind her was a man in an old-fashioned pinstriped suit and pale green shirt open at the chest to show the twinkling of a gold medallion. He had a long grey beard and was wearing what could only be described as a gangster's hat. His lower half was wrapped in a blanket. Finally there was a young girl with her hair in bunches wearing a long blue bridesmaid's dress. She must be their daughter thought the residents as she smiled up at them, showing off a chipped front tooth. They were all awfully pale – perhaps their condition was hereditary.

'It's a pleasure to meet you,' Albert was saying, shaking Mr Harris by the hand. 'It's an honour to be here at last.'

Mr Harris, still speechless, prized his hand out of Albert's cold grip and wiped it surreptitiously on his thigh – but not before noticing Albert's gold medallion, and the jewels round Gaynor's neck.

'It's everything we thought it would be, and more,' said Gaynor, taking Mr Harris's other hand. She bit her lip and looked about, noting the regal (if threadbare) red carpets, the cut glass door handles and the dusty chandelier. 'Beautiful!' she said, her voice breaking. 'Beautiful!'

The residents exchanged amused glances.

'Check this out, Mum!' yelled Eliza, wheeling through into the dining room.

Her parents followed and there came cries of 'Goodness!' and 'Fantastic!' and when the residents crept down the stairs and peered round the doorway they were astonished to see the Flots wheeling between the tables examining the cups and salt shakers. The residents nudged each other, and raised their eyebrows.

'Excuse me!' said Mr Harris. 'Hey! Come

out of there!'

But before he could stride after the Flots there came a shout: 'Kenneth!' and there was Margot standing regally at the top of the stairs. She was all dressed for breakfast in a red jumper with a brooch on it, and a kilt and sensible shoes.

'Margot!' said Mr Harris. 'W–what are *you* doing out of bed?'

'I'm meeting my friends for breakfast. Bring us a pot of tea, would you, Kenneth? And use the best china.'

Mr Harris hesitated. He had always been a little intimidated by Margot ever since they were children, but he would never admit it. She was older than him and once, when he had refused to lend her a book, she had wrestled it off him and bent back his little finger so hard that he had had to wear a special finger sling for a week. He glanced towards the dining room. 'They're *friends* of yours?'

'They are indeed,' said Margot, making her way downstairs and thunking her cane on every step. 'Oh – and would you bring their bags in, please?' And she swept past him into the dining room.

'Bags? What bags?' said Mr Harris. Then his mouth fell open. Stacked just outside he noticed several old chests that looked as though they had just been dredged up from the bottom of the ocean.

The residents glanced at each other as if to say 'just this once', and tidying their bedtime hair and adjusting the belts of their robes they shuffled into the dining room, giggling nervously.

Breakfast was not the hushed affair that it normally was. There was an air of festivity in the dining room that morning. For once, Toby was not the only one in his pyjamas as he rushed about the dining room serving tea and toast – and Margot was seated at breakfast for the first time since anyone could remember. She and the Captain sat at the Flots' table and showed them how to crack their eggs with a spoon and butter their toast, and Toby was kept busy running to and fro for extra jam and wiping up bits of food with a damp cloth.

'However did you get the wheelchairs down to the beach for us?' asked Gaynor. She had given up on spreading the butter, and was eating it instead with a teaspoon.

'The Captain was a marvellous help,' said Margot.

The Captain swelled with pride. 'It wasn't easy,' he said. 'I had to wheel Margot down to the beach three times – as a cover-up, you see – then we'd leave the chair under the pier and she'd hobble back on her sticks.'

'I'm sure I didn't *hobble*,' said Margot crisply. To the others, she said: 'If anyone had seen us I would have told them I was trying out new chairs.'

'Sand was the problem,' recalled the Captain. 'She was *such* a heavy load, and the wheels really *dig in* and—'

'How do you like your dress, Eliza?' Margot said briskly as Mr Harris appeared suddenly with an enormous china teapot.

'Lovely,' said Eliza with her mouth full.

Breakfast took longer that morning. None of the residents seemed to want to go and get dressed – the new guests were far too entertaining. Margot started telling the Flots about the time she had seen a mermaid singing. 'I was just a girl,' she said. 'But I remember it as though it was yesterday.' And she began to sing: *'Morning has broken, like the first morning…!'*

Gaynor laid down her knife and fork and sang the next line in a high, clear voice: *'Blackbird has spoken, like the first bird!'*

Margot gasped. 'It was *you*? You were the mermaid on the rock that day?'

Gaynor smiled, and together she and Margot sang the rest of the song, and one by one all the residents in the dining room joined in, too. Albert and the Captain applauded when it was over, but Mr Harris just muttered something about 'too early for singing', and went back to bed.

But eventually breakfast was finished and the residents pushed back their chairs and trooped upstairs again talking and laughing, and by the time the Flots finally wiped their sticky fingers and pushed away their plates they were the only ones left in the room. There was food all over the tablecloth, egg down their fronts, and Eliza had a blob of marmalade hanging in her hair.

'I thought you did very well,' said Toby, clearing the plates. 'For the first time in a proper restaurant.'

'You're too kind!' said Gaynor, licking her knife.

Margot and the Captain rose from the table. 'We'll leave you to get settled in,' said Margot. 'Mrs Harris will show you to room 11. But I feel I must warn you . . .' and here she glanced about and lowered her voice. 'It's about Mr Harris,' she said. 'He runs this place with a rod of iron – and he's not to be trusted.'

'She's right,' said Toby. 'Try and keep a low profile.'

'Don't you worry about a thing,' said Albert, patting Toby's hand. 'He'll never even know we're here.'

Chapter 13

But it was not easy for the Flots to keep a low profile, and that first early breakfast was only the start of many disruptions to the daily routine at The Grand. On the second morning Mr Harris came downstairs to find that all the tables and chairs had been moved outside so that the residents could watch the sun rise while they had their breakfast.

'What's going on here?' he said when he saw it.

'We're watching the sun,' said Margot, who was sipping tea with the rest of them. 'Come and join us. And you, Nigel.'

Mr Harris glowered and gritted his teeth, but what could he say when all the residents (still wearing their dressing gowns and slippers) were raising their teacups to him and wishing him a good morning? After a moment's hesitation he turned on his heel and stalked away, and Nigel hurried after him.

During the day, while everyone else was digging for treasure, Gaynor and Cook enjoyed tea and sandwiches on the promenade. Albert played poker with the residents until the wind got up and blew the Ace of Spades into the sea, and Toby wheeled Eliza down the pier. Eliza bought them both ice cream and postcards, and she exchanged her opal pendant for one of those glass balls that snow inside when you tip them up. Except that inside this ball was a mermaid with real hair that wafted this way and that in the water, and instead of snow there was a shoal of silver fishes that fluttered all around her.

'There you are!' said Mr Harris when he saw Toby. 'Get back inside this minute. Go and clean the toilets.'

'He's cleaned them already,' said Eliza cheerfully, 'so I've hired him to wheel me around.'

'You've *hired* him?'

'Yep,' said Eliza, and she pulled a string of pearls out of a little embroidered purse that she wore around her neck and waggled it at Mr Harris.

'I'll take that,' said Mr Harris, snatching it rudely, 'on behalf of my employee.'

Eliza laughed. 'I thought you might,' she said.

Mr Harris pocketed the pearls greedily, and watched as Toby wheeled Eliza off. That boy was having too much fun, he reckoned. That wasn't *work*. And why should Toby be enjoying himself when here *he* was, burdened with responsibility? That boy was lucky that he let him work at his hotel at all – having a good time as well was just *too much*.

Then, to top it off, the Flots started a choir. Every evening at seven o'clock when the dinner had been cleared away, the residents gathered in the dining room to sing. They all stood in rows while Gaynor sat at the front conducting, and their voices could be heard floating out of the open windows and right down the promenade – songs about sunken treasure and shipwrecked sailors and women waiting on the shore for ships that never came in. Margot and the Captain were the loudest; they both stood at the front trying to outdo each other. Toby and Eliza always went to the back and giggled and sucked sweets, but nobody minded. Even Mrs Harris and Cook joined in. And though he couldn't be persuaded to sing, Nigel often sat on the stairs, listening.

'I wish they'd stop that wailing,' muttered Mr Harris. He had taken to plugging his ears with cotton wool. Their singing gave him the shivers, he said – and it wasn't the only thing that did. Something wasn't *right* about those Flots, he decided. He would have turned them out ages ago had it not been for all the jewellery they kept flashing about – and paying him with. They were a very disruptive influence. They were so ready to *enjoy* themselves, and somehow wherever they went everyone else had fun as well. Even Margot was out of bed again. For the first time in years, The Grand was filled with laughter and the babble of conversation. And Mr Harris didn't like it. He didn't like it one bit.

He cornered Mrs Harris on the third floor one afternoon while she was making beds. 'Emily,' he said, 'do you notice anything – how shall I put it – *odd* about the new guests?'

Mrs Harris stopped and thought. 'Well,' she said, 'they do use an awful lot of towels.'

'Oh?'

'Yes. And they leave a lot of sand in the bath.'

'Really . . .' said Mr Harris thoughtfully.

'Yes. And there's another thing, too . . .'

'Yes? What's that?' asked Mr Harris, leaning in eagerly.

'Well,' she said, 'they're always so. . .

happy.' And with that, she turned on her heel and bustled off down the corridor.

Mr Harris was just heading back towards the lift when Toby came along, holding a tall stack of towels for the Flots' room. 'Ah!' said Mr Harris, blocking the corridor. 'Towels for the Flots, is it?'

Toby said nothing, just stared at Mr Harris over the top of the towels.

'Why do they need more towels than anyone else, then? Tell me that, eh? And tell me another thing,' he said, before Toby could answer. 'What's *wrong* with them?'

'What?'

'What's wrong with the Flots?'

Toby's eyes widened. 'Nothing's wrong with them!' he stammered.

'Is that right?' Mr Harris peered at Toby as though he was able see right inside his head. 'Yes, I thought as much. There's nothing wrong with them at all, is there? They're only pretending.'

'No!'

'Yes,' said Mr Harris. 'They just want
everyone to feel *sorry* for them, don't they?
They want everyone to run about after them,
pandering to their every need! Well, jewels or
no jewels, I won't be made a fool of!' And
with that he turned and walked away,
muttering as he went: 'I knew it! I knew
there was something fishy about that lot.
Something very fishy indeed . . .'

Chapter 14

That night Nigel was up late watching
television in his room when he heard
the front door shut with a bang. Who could be
going out at this time of night? He went to the
window, parted the curtains, and looked out.

To his astonishment Nigel saw three chairs
going down the ramp in single file. The Flots!
And right behind them Nigel recognized
Margot with her swimming-cap on, the
Captain with a towel draped round his
shoulders, and Toby wearing only his pyjama
bottoms. The party made their way across the
sand and disappeared behind the bulkhead
of the pier.

For a long while Nigel stood at the

window but the chairs did not re-appear. The waves just kept washing in and out as though nothing had happened. Had he imagined it? He began to feel cold, and the hairs rose on the back of his neck. Perhaps he should go and wake his dad? But then, what if there was no one down there?

With a beating heart Nigel crept downstairs and out of the hotel, letting the front door close softly behind him. All was quiet. He tiptoed down the ramp and on to the beach and followed the dark runnels that the wheels had left in the sand. The tracks went right down to the water's edge, and there they were – the three chairs – standing in a row at the black lip of the ocean, the metal glinting in the moonlight.

They were empty.

With his heart pounding, Nigel approached the chairs. Folded neatly on the seats he found three bathrobes with *The Grand* embroidered on the pockets. There was not a soul in sight, just the unceasing rhythm of the waves, in and out, in and out . . .

Then suddenly there was a squeal of laughter (could that be *Toby?*) a muffled shout and a splash, and Nigel noticed six heads bobbing in the shadows beneath the pier. He was just about to announce his presence by shouting 'I'm telling Dad!' when one of the heads ducked beneath the water and in its place a large fluked tail appeared, and then was gone again.

With a strangled cry Nigel turned around and staggered up the beach, his feet slowed by the wet sand like in a dream where you can't run fast enough. He pounded up the ramp and flung himself against the front door of the hotel. It was locked! 'Mum!' shrieked Nigel, rattling the handle furiously. 'Mum!'

Lights started to go on in the rooms. People came out on to the landing, wrapping their bathrobes about them and rubbing their eyes. Nigel pressed his thumb on the doorbell and kept it there.

Eventually the front door flew open and there was Mr Harris looking furious in his dressing gown and slippers. Without a word

he seized Nigel by the collar, dragged him inside and slammed the door. Once again all was quiet outside save for the sound of waves breaking on the beach.

'But, Dad,' insisted Nigel, 'I'm not making it up!' He was close to tears now.

'What's wrong with you?' said his father coldly. 'I thought you'd outgrown these imaginary friends and these childish stories about fairies and—'

'Not *fairies*,' shouted Nigel. 'Mermaids.'

'Don't you raise your voice to me, young man. Haven't I told you before?'

Nigel tried to keep his chin from quivering.

'Haven't I?' repeated his father, tilting Nigel's face towards him.

'Yes,' said Nigel, blinking the tears from his eyes.

'Good. Get back to bed, then.'

When Mr Harris returned to his room he found Mrs Harris sitting up in bed examining something under the bedside lamp.

'Those Flots have gone too far this time,' he muttered, taking off his dressing gown. 'Night swimming! And the sign clearly says not to take towels or bathrobes out of the rooms.'

But Mrs Harris wasn't listening. She was turning the object over and over in her fingers.

'Look what I found,' she said. 'Can I have it as a pendant?' And she held it up for him to see.

The light shone right through it. It was a translucent blue-green disk, like a giant tiddly-wink, or a sequin, or an enormous . . .

'It's a fish scale,' said Mr Harris slowly.

Mrs Harris turned the scale this way and that. She put it to her eye and looked at Mr Harris through it. 'Pretty big for a fish,' she remarked.

'Where did you find it?' demanded Mr Harris.

'There's no need to snatch!'

'I said where did you find it?' Mr Harris repeated.

'In room 11,' said Mrs Harris, sulkily.
'Why?'

'Nothing,' said Mr Harris, and he slipped
the blue disc into his pyjama pocket, got into
bed, and turned off the light.

Chapter 15

During the night another cruise ship had arrived. The *Queen Canute* had come ashore with storm damage, and would be docked until the following day. There was a tap tap tapping in the background as workmen hammered at the hull from a hanging platform.

Margot and the Captain and Toby were sitting on the pier with the Flots. They were discussing the mysterious trail of footsteps they had found leading down the beach to the Flots' wheelchairs after their midnight swim.

'Perhaps there's someone spying on us,' said Gaynor.

'Even if there was,' said Eliza, 'they probably didn't recognize us.'

'But what if they did?'

'I don't care,' said Eliza recklessly.

'Well, you should,' said Gaynor. 'What they might do to us doesn't bear thinking about. I heard of one old dear – before you were born, it was. Apparently they put her on a leash and made her dive for fish. Imagine!'

'Your mother is right,' said Margot. 'We've got to be careful.'

'Perhaps,' said the Captain cautiously, 'it would be safer to go back.'

'Back where? To the cave?' cried Eliza. 'No! I *won't!*'

They all looked towards the beach. There were still a few people digging for treasure, and from a small boat anchored offshore divers were searching the seabed.

'I'm not sure it's any safer out there,' said Toby.

Just then, as if to prove it, there was a sudden commotion beneath the pier. 'I wonder what's going on?' said Margot. They hurried to the railings and looked down to see a procession of divers wearing head torches and rubber gloves coming out from beneath the pier. Each of them was carrying something.

'Is it the treasure?' shouted an onlooker.

'More like rubbish,' answered another.

But the Flots looked on in horror when they saw what it was that the frogmen were carrying: the battered buoy that Gaynor used as a bolster, Albert's hammock cut down and bundled into a ball, all the chipped china . . .

'My doll!' yelled Eliza, before Gaynor was able to clap her hand over her daughter's mouth.

Everything was put into plastic bags and sealed and then the frogmen marched back for more.

'Well,' said Albert, 'we can't go back *there* again.'

Nobody spoke, and the tap-tap-tapping of the workmen on the cruise ship rang out in the silence.

'What will you do now?' asked the Captain.

Gaynor sighed. 'I think we'll have to go away,' she said. 'Lie low for a while.'

'I don't want to go away!' said Eliza. 'I want to stay at The Grand.'

'I'm afraid your mother's right, Eliza,' said Albert. 'Just until things settle down.' And he began to cough as though his chest was already beginning to feel the damp again.

'This is all my fault,' said Toby. 'If only I'd hidden the ring!'

'Don't say that,' said Gaynor, putting her cold hand on Toby's. 'We've had the time of our lives, and we always knew we couldn't stay for ever.'

Toby sighed, and tears pricked his eyes. Everything had been so much *better* since the Flots had arrived. They were like the family he'd never had. If they went away again everything would go back to how it was before. There would be no more singing or night swimming or picnicking or any of the things they had been doing these last few days. And Margot might go back to bed.

'If only there was somewhere *else* we

could go,' said Gaynor to no one in particular. 'Somewhere no one would recognize us.'

Behind them the *Queen Canute* sat waiting at the end of the pier. Toby looked at the workmen hanging at the side of the hull. Tap-tap-tap went their hammers. Tomorrow the ship would sail away again; it was the last boat of the season. Summer was drawing to an end and Toby felt suddenly lonely as though the Flots had already gone. Then he grew thoughtful. 'Maybe,' he said slowly, 'there *is* somewhere. And then, when everything is quiet you could come back again . . .'

'Where?' said Eliza.

'I know the tickets won't be cheap,' said Toby cautiously, 'and we'll have to act quickly – but it *could* be just what you're looking for. If we could find the money . . .'

'Tickets?' said Margot. 'Tickets for what?'

Toby glanced round to make sure that no one was listening. 'It's just an idea,' he said, 'and it won't be easy, but here's my plan . . .'

Meanwhile, Nigel sat slumped in the high-backed chair watching television. At least, his eyes were goggling at the screen but his mind was elsewhere. 'And here we are,' said a voice on the television. 'Live at the scene of the latest discovery . . .'

Nigel blinked and sat up. He had recognized the beach outside The Grand. Behind the presenter divers plodded past carrying various objects – a buoy, a china teapot, an old doll.

'. . . valuable silverware,' went on the presenter, 'undoubtedly from the same haul as the Duke's ring. But the big question is: Who has been living here? And why?'

'Dad!' hollered Nigel.

Mr Harris came and stood behind Nigel's chair.

'Officer,' said the presenter, angling the fuzzy microphone at a policeman holding a plastic bag, 'can you tell us what you've got there?'

The camera zoomed in on the bag. In one corner there was a sort of a round disc, shimmery green, like an enormous sequin.

'It's a scale,' said the policeman.

'Pretty big for a scale,' said the presenter.

'Indeed,' said the policeman. 'Experts are trying to determine which species it belongs to.'

Then the camera zoomed out again and showed the presenter and the policeman standing on the rocky shore with The Grand Hotel behind.

'From The Grand Hotel, this is James Thorn,' said the presenter.

Nigel pointed the remote control at the TV and switched it off. 'See?' he said. 'I *told* you.'

But Mr Harris had taken from his pocket the disc-like object that his wife had found and was rotating it slowly between his fingers. 'Hmmm . . .' he said thoughtfully.

'It was the Flots, Dad,' said Nigel. 'The Flots lived there.'

Mr Harris put the scale to his eye and looked at Nigel through it. Nigel jumped. Through the glassy disc his father's eye was large and ogling, like a fish's.

'Aha!' cried Mr Harris. 'I've got it!'

'Got what?'

'Follow me,' said Mr Harris, turning on his heel and marching from the room, 'and you'll see.'

Nigel loitered uneasily outside room 11 while his father set about the peephole with his screwdriver.

'Dad!' he hissed. 'What if someone sees you?'

'Shut up, Nigel,' snapped his father. And presently, with a shower of sawdust, the little round lens popped out of the door and went rolling across the floor.

'Drat!' said Mr Harris, feeling over the carpet on his hands and knees. 'Get down here and help me. I've lost it.'

They both groped about in the corridor.

'There it is!' cried Mr Harris, pouncing. And while Nigel kept a furtive lookout, Mr Harris screwed the fish eye lens back into the door *the wrong way round*.

'There we are,' he said at last, clapping the

dust off his hands and putting his eye to the hole. 'Splendid! Ha-ha! I can see everything – the bed, the armoire, those ugly chests. When they get back I'll—'

Just then there was the 'bing!' of the lift. The doors slid open and out wheeled the Flots, followed by Toby, Margot and the Captain.

'Uh – hello!' stuttered Mr Harris. 'Not out enjoying the sun then?'

'Hello, Mr Harris!' said Gaynor. 'Hello, Nigel! We were just saying how nice it is to be able to enjoy the privacy of your own room sometimes.'

'Quite, quite,' said Mr Harris. He grinned ingratiatingly as they all filed in. 'Make yourselves at home.'

Toby glanced at Mr Harris suspiciously, but he didn't notice the screwdriver in his hand. And he didn't notice the scattering of sawdust on the carpet, either. When they had all gone in Mr Harris closed the door, glanced up and down the corridor and put his eye to the peephole.

'What do you see, Dad?' hissed Nigel.

Mr Harris's eye was glued to the door.

'Dad?'

Mr Harris did not reply, but with a look of horror on his face, he slowly backed away from room 11. Then he turned and fled. Down the hall he ran, straight past the lift and – crash! – through the fire exit and on to the fire escape. Round and down the spiral stairway he rushed, with Nigel coming quickly after him, Mr Harris taking the stairs three at a time with his jacket flapping out behind. Into the back yard, through the kitchen door, and down the hall to the front lounge.

At the bar Mr Harris poured himself a tumbler of brandy with shaking hands and took a big swig. 'Fish!' he said. '*Fish* in room 11! And you should see the *jewels* they've got – all those chests are full of booty! The others are in on it, too. Toby and Margot were right there, standing as close as you are now and chatting away as if nothing was wrong.' He shuddered. 'I'll never forget it,' he said. 'That awful woman with her skirt up round her waist and that – *tail* – on the footstool.'

Nigel climbed up onto the barstool next to his father. 'I told you, Dad,' he said, 'but you–'

'I'm going to be rich,' said Mr Harris suddenly. 'And famous. They're going to say I've made the greatest discovery of the century!'

'But it was me who dis–'

'You know, Nigel,' said Mr Harris, turning on him suddenly, 'it's about time people took me seriously. Gave me the respect I deserve. You think I like being stuck in this dump? You think I *like* my job?'

'Um . . .'

'Well, I don't,' said Mr Harris. 'I've never been appreciated. I–'

Just then he was interrupted by the 'bing!' of the lift out in the hall. They heard the doors open and voices approaching. Quickly, Mr Harris and Nigel ducked down behind the bar and waited until the front door slammed. They popped their heads up just in time to see the Flots wheeling off down the road with Toby and the Captain.

'I wonder where they're going?' said Nigel.

'Well, wherever it is,' said his father bitterly, 'they'd better make the most of it – while they still can.'

'Why? What are you going to do, Dad?'

Mr Harris looked at Nigel and smiled. Nigel jumped. He thought how it was funny that smiling made most people look nicer, but not his father. Perhaps it was just as well that his father rarely smiled. Come to think of it Nigel couldn't remember ever having seen his father smile before. Oh, yes he could – that time that Nigel had got his hair caught in the fan. His father had laughed then.

'I'm going to EXHIBIT them,' said Mr Harris. 'They'll be on TV in every household in the country tomorrow.' He laughed. 'And so shall I! I'll travel the world giving interviews.'

'But what about me and Mum?'

Mr Harris's smile faded, and he regarded Nigel coldly.

'You're always thinking about yourself, aren't you, Nigel? It's always me-me-me with you, isn't it? Well, now it's *my* turn.'

Chapter 16

A little bell rang as the party entered the jewellery shop, and the woman behind the counter looked up. There stood the Captain twisting his cap in his hands and Toby standing shyly beside him with bare feet. Behind them the Flots were exclaiming loudly about the high ceilings and impressive chandeliers.

'I'm afraid there's no browsing allowed,' said the woman sharply. 'We can only accommodate those who want to *buy*.' And she looked at them pointedly.

Toby's face fell, and he and the Captain conferred quickly with the Flots.

'Leave it to me,' said Albert, and he wheeled up to the counter, followed closely by Gaynor. 'Well, we don't want to *buy*,' he said loudly, 'we want to *sell*.'

Gaynor opened a satin pouch and tipped the jewels into her lap. The jewels glowed as though with a light of their own and cast ripples of colour over the ceiling. The woman gasped. Gaynor lifted a tangle of necklaces. 'We'd like to get rid of some of these trinkets,' she said.

The woman moved her mouth like a fish, but no sound came out.

'But never mind,' said Albert, backing up and turning his wheelchair around. 'We'll try elsewhere.'

'Oh!' cried the woman, flapping. 'Just a moment. Let me talk to Mr Newton! Wait right there!' and she went rushing into the back and returned a moment later with an old gentlemen in a black suit.

'I'm Mr Newton,' said the old man. 'How can I help?' He wore a monocle and a small moustache and had very long yellow hands that he rubbed together constantly.

Gaynor held up a string of blue sapphires that winked and twinkled under the lights. Mr Newton reached for the necklace but before he could get his hands on it Gaynor had dropped it back into her lap again, saying: 'Sorry, can't let you have that one. My mother teethed me on that.' And she began rooting through the loot again while the lady and Mr Newton craned their necks to get a better look.

'There's this old thing,' Gaynor said, fishing out a velvet choker with an enormous diamond at the front. But just as Mr Newton reached out for it she snatched it back again, saying: 'No – sorry, I'd feel bad letting that one go. My sister Sheryl used to put that one on her pet seal.'

Gaynor delved into the tangle once more. 'Look at that!' she cried suddenly, holding up a ruby the size of a cherry and rolling it between her fingers.

Mr Newton gasped.

'So it was here all the time!' said Gaynor,

dropping the ruby back again.

'Aha!' she said at last, fishing out a string of black pearls. 'We don't mind seeing the back of that one, do we, Eliza?'

Eliza blushed. '*Mum!*' she said.

'Well I'll be darned,' said Albert, looking on. 'We never thought that would see the light of day again, did we, love?' and he and Gaynor laughed. 'Eliza swallowed it when she was three,' he said.

The lady, who had been reaching out to take the necklace, drew back quickly and brought out a pair of rubber gloves. She and Mr Newton were soon bent over it with magnifying glasses.

'Perfect, quite perfect,' breathed Mr Newton.

Toby smiled at the Captain and turned to the jewellers. 'So,' he said boldly. 'How much is it worth?'

Meanwhile, back at The Grand the dinner bell went.

'Tell Cook there'll be five less for dinner,' Margot told Mrs Harris. 'The Captain and Toby have gone to town with the Flots.'

Just then Mr Harris came staggering out of the bar. He was waving his glass in the air calling 'Champagne! Bring me champagne!'

'Make it six less,' remarked Margot, dryly.

Mrs Harris hurried to remove the glass.

'He wouldn't stop,' said Nigel, trailing his father helplessly.

'Better get him up to bed,' said Margot.

So Nigel and Mrs Harris each took an arm, and between them managed to help Mr Harris up the stairs.

'Champagne?' said one of the residents. 'That's not like him.'

'No,' said Margot, frowning. 'It's *most* unusual . . .' But no sooner had Mr Harris gone upstairs than the Flots sailed through the front door, beaming. Albert was waving three gold tickets in the air.

'We're off,' he announced. 'We're setting sail tomorrow on the *Queen Canute*!'

Chapter 17

The next morning the dining room was loud with breakfast chatter. The *Queen Canute* was ready to depart and the passengers were enjoying one last cake and cup of tea with the residents of The Grand. Toby was busy stacking cases in the corridor.

Mr Harris staggered downstairs clutching his head. 'I'll be in my office,' he growled. 'And I *will not be disturbed.*' And in he went, slamming the door so hard that it left the wall shaking. A moment later he popped his head out. 'Unless it's the gentlemen for Operation Fish,' he said, and slammed the door again.

Mrs Harris sighed and wrote 'Operation Fish' in the book – whatever that might mean.

A moment later Nigel came down, yawning.

'Morning,' said Mrs Harris.

Nigel had just opened his mouth to reply when he noticed a pile of crusty old chests stacked in the corridor. 'What are they doing there?' he asked his mother. 'Don't they belong to the Flots?'

'Haven't you heard?' said Mrs Harris. 'The Flots are leaving today.'

'Leaving? What do you mean – *leaving*?'

'They're leaving on the boat, Nigel,' said his mother patiently. 'They bought their tickets yesterday. They're going on a cruise and won't be back until next summer.'

Just then Eliza came wheeling round the corner. She was wearing a large blue hat with a white ribbon round it, and her hair was in curls. She was waving a piece of toast. 'Nigel!' she said. 'I was just looking for you!'

'You were?' Nigel took a step back.

'Yes,' said Eliza, and she wheeled right up to him and pulled him down in a hug. 'Bye!' she said, then she let him go and wheeled back into the dining room.

Nigel stared after her for a long moment. Then he marched down the hall to his father's office and knocked on the door.

'Dad?' he said.

'What?' snapped his father without looking up from his papers.

Nigel sidled in and hovered before the desk. 'It's about the Flots,' he said.

'It's all in hand,' said Mr Harris. 'You don't need to concern yourself.'

'But . . .'

'I said it's all under control,' said Mr Harris sharply. 'When I get a minute's peace I'll make some calls. It takes careful planning, you know, an operation like this.'

'A what?' said Nigel.

But Mr Harris ignored him. He was making notes on bits of paper as he spoke, and sticking them here and there about his desk. 'As soon as the boat has gone and the guests have cleared out,' he was saying, 'the fun will begin . . .'

'Fun?'

'I nearly forgot,' muttered Mr Harris. 'I'll need to call the TV network.'

Nigel paled.

'Press, police, television people . . .' Mr Harris was scribbling notes, shuffling papers. 'The Flots will be on TV in every household in the country before the end of the day. We'll have people lining up to see those freaks. We'll need to concrete the beach for parking. Do you think it's in good taste to take their clothes away?'

Nigel looked on helplessly as his father scribbled 'security guards' in his notebook. So *this* was what his father had been planning! He was going to collect money from people who wanted to gawp at the Flots, and who knows what else? Make them do circus tricks, perhaps? And then when people had tired of it, he could sell the Flots for scientific research.

Mr Harris glanced up at Nigel. 'Go on,' he

said, waving him away. 'Go and make yourself useful.'

Nigel didn't move. 'Dad,' he said bravely, 'I don't think the Flots would like being exhibited.'

There was a pause.

Mr Harris took of his spectacles and looked at Nigel as if he was seeing him for the first time. 'Who cares?' he said. 'They're only *fish*. Now go on – get out!'

Nigel looked at his father for a long moment. Then he turned and walked out, closing the door softly behind him.

Outside everyone was milling about in the corridor. The passengers from the cruise ship were collecting their coats and Toby was hurrying to and fro with bags and cases.

'Farewell, Nigel!' said Albert, wheeling up to Nigel and shaking him firmly by the hand. 'Where's your dad?'

'Er – he's in his office,' said Nigel.

'Oh good. We'll go and say goodbye,' said Albert.

'No!' said Nigel quickly. 'He can't be disturbed. I'll say it for you.'

'Thanks, Nigel,' said Gaynor. 'Tell him we've had a lovely time.' And she planted a chilly wet kiss on the boy's cheek.

'Come on,' said Toby anxiously. 'You'll miss the boat.' He moved behind Eliza's chair and set off down the corridor – but coming through the door were several men. Two of them carried cameras, and the rest wore long beige coats and had notebooks tucked under their arms.

'I say,' said the Captain. 'Who's this?'

'It's Mr Wallace from the Weekly News,' said Margot in surprise, 'and his reporters. What are they doing here?'

The men marched up to the reception desk. 'Operation Fish,' said one, and Mrs Harris jumped out from behind the desk and rapped on the office door. Mr Harris popped his head out. 'Ah! Here you are,' he said. 'Perfect! I'm on the phone to the coastguard now, and . . .' He stopped when he noticed the Flots in the hall. 'And where are *you* all going?' he said.

'To the boat!' said Gaynor brightly. 'It's departing. We just wanted to say—'

'Oh, the boat, the boat,' said Mr Harris impatiently. 'I don't see why *everyone* has to go and say goodbye.'

Gaynor smiled and wheeled over to squeeze his hand. 'It's all right,' she said. 'Goodbyes are hard for everyone.'

Mr Harris pulled his hand away. 'Well come back soon,' he snapped, and retreated into his office with the reporters.

Gaynor watched him go fondly. 'Did you hear that?' she said. 'He's going to miss us. He wants us to come back soon!'

Toby and Margot exchanged a dubious look but before they could say anything in came Police Constable Brick followed by a man with a rifle and the dogcatcher carrying a large net. They too marched straight up to the reception desk then joined the others in the office.

The ship's horn blasted once, twice.

'Now!' said Toby urgently. 'It's time to go.'

And he wheeled Eliza over the threshold. The Captain followed quickly with Gaynor and Albert.

Margot was still waving goodbye from the front door when she felt something tugging at her sleeve. 'Nigel!' she said. 'What's the matter?'

Nigel's eyes were round and his face worried. 'It's my dad,' he whispered. 'You've got to stop him.'

Chapter 18

In the office the photographers tinkered with their equipment, the reporters muttered, and Constable Brick rocked impatiently on his heels.

'Mr Harris,' said Constable Brick eventually, 'I'm not a man with a lot of time. Why did you ask us all to come? And why the secrecy?'

Mr Harris rapped on his desk and waited for everyone to settle. Then he cleared his throat. 'Before we begin,' he said, 'I must ask you to refrain from taking photographs. I'll be happy to oblige you later, in the—'

'Get on with it!' said someone at the back.

Mr Harris ignored the interruption. 'As

you're all aware,' he went on, 'I announced the discovery of the Duke's ring.'

There were grumbles from around the room, and people rolled their eyes.

'And now,' continued Mr Harris, 'I'm pleased to announce that I've also discovered the rest of the Duke's jewels!'

Instantly everyone jumped to their feet and started talking at once.

'Quiet, please!' said Mr Harris.

They fell silent.

'That's not the best part,' said Mr Harris, smiling. 'I've also identified the individuals who *found* the treasure.'

Everyone looked around expectantly.

Mr Harris gave a small smile. 'Gentlemen,' he said, 'what I am about to tell you may sound incredible. What I am about to tell you may sound—'

'Just tell us!' barked someone, and there was laughter.

Mr Harris took a deep breath. 'The finders of the lost treasure,' he said, 'are *mermaids*.'

There was a heavy silence.

'*You* know,' said Mr Harris in rather a high voice. 'Scales? Tail like a fish? Makes sense, doesn't it? Mermaids can dive for sunken treasure better than anyone!'

'You're trying to tell us,' said Constable Brick, 'that the finders of the Duke's lost treasure are a bunch of *mermaids?*'

'Three,' said Mr Harris weakly. 'Just three.'

At that very moment the Flots were heading down the pier.

'All aboard!' shouted Albert, his bony arms pumping like pistons as he sailed straight up the gangplank and disappeared into the bowels of the ship.

Gaynor came next, pushed by the Captain. She was blowing kisses to the crowd and alternately waving her handkerchief and dabbing at her eyes with it. At the top of the ramp she pressed the Captain's hand to her lips, gave the crowd one last queenly wave and disappeared. The Captain hurried back down the ramp again.

A tearful Cook gave Eliza a cream bun in

a brown paper bag and then Toby pushed her chair to the top of the ramp.

'We'll miss you,' said Eliza, and she pulled Toby down into a fierce hug.

'I'll miss you, too,' said Toby.

'Oh!' said Eliza. 'I nearly forgot. I want you to have this.' And she reached into her purse and pulled out a heavy round globe – the mermaid in the glass ball – and handed it to Toby.

The ship's horn blasted one last time.

'Thanks for everything,' said Eliza.

'Goodbye!' said Toby in a strangled voice, and he turned and rushed back down the gangplank clutching the glass ball. Just in time! The moment he jumped down on to the pier the gangplank was drawn up, the ropes were untied, and the *Queen Canute* pulled slowly away. And there were the Flots, waving from the top deck.

'Watch you don't roll overboard!' shouted the Captain through cupped hands. 'And remember what I told you about being seasick – just look at the horizon!'

'Don't forget to eat!' called Cook, waving a handkerchief.

'We'll send postcards!' yelled Eliza. She was already eating Cook's cream bun and her mouth was full. 'We'll see you next summer!'

Back at the hotel, Margot and Nigel were listening at the office door. From within there came sounds of movement. Chairs were being scraped back and people were getting up. The reporters were snapping their notebooks closed and the photographers packing their cameras.

'Some people – they'll do anything to get in the papers,' said one of the reporters.

'Wait!' came Mr Harris's voice. 'I'll prove it!'

'Not if I can help it,' muttered Margot, and she flung open the door.

Everyone stopped and turned to look. 'There!' cried Mr Harris, pointing. '*She* can tell you! Ask *her*!'

The photographers and reporters exchanged looks. Constable Brick cleared his throat uncomfortably. 'Is this true?' he asked.

'Have you seen these . . . mermaids?'

Margot and Nigel glanced round the room and met the curious stares. The reporters held their pens ready, the photographers waited.

Margot gave a little laugh. 'Mermaids?' she said. 'Surely people don't believe in mermaids any more?'

Mr Harris turned purple and pointed an accusing finger. 'They're *friends* of hers!' he spluttered.

'I think Mr Harris is referring to the Flots,' said Margot helpfully. 'They were guests at the hotel. In wheelchairs.'

Constable Brick frowned at Mr Harris.

'Nigel!' cried Mr Harris. 'Tell them what *you* saw!'

Nigel's chin trembled and he looked at the carpet. 'You said you didn't want any more childish nonsense,' he said, which was true enough.

Constable Brick regarded Mr Harris sternly. 'I think, Mr Harris, you're a little overwrought,' he said.

Mr Harris let out a strangled yowl. 'I'll show you! You'll see!' And before anyone could stop him he had rushed from the room. The reporter and photographers hurried after him.

They found Mr Harris in the TV room tossing the sofa cushions onto the floor as though he might find the Flots hiding beneath them.

'Kenneth!' cried Margot.

Mr Harris took no notice but rushed across the hall into the dining room and ran between the tables, lifting the cloths and peering between the table legs. The Flots were not there either. He dashed out into the hall and looked left and right. His hair was frantic now, and a mauve vein was standing out at his temple. Suddenly he turned on Margot and Nigel. 'Where are they?' he yelled.

Margot shrugged. 'They've gone,' she said.

'GONE?'

With a strangled cry, Mr Harris lunged forward and seized Margot by the throat. She let out a squawk.

'Now, now,' said Constable Brick, stepping forward and wrestling Mr Harris's arms behind his back.

'GONE WHERE?' shrieked Mr Harris, struggling. And then, as if in reply, the ship's horn sounded one last time. Mr Harris froze. 'THE BOAT!' he shouted and, flailing his arms like windmills, he broke free and rushed headlong down the hall and out of the front door. He ran down the pier and flung himself against the railings. 'Stop them!' he cried. 'They're getting away!'

But passengers on the departing ship continued to wave gaily, and Albert, who had his binoculars out, said suddenly: 'Oh look! It's Mr Harris! He's come to see us off!'

'So it is!' said Gaynor. 'Wave, everyone!' and they all waved back merrily and shouted 'Goodbye!'

'Come back!' yelled Mr Harris.

'Someone had better stop him,' said Margot. 'He looks like he's going to – oh!' For even as she spoke Mr Harris had put one shiny shoe on to the lower railing, and was throwing his other leg over the top.

'Dad!' cried Nigel. But the next moment Mr Harris, tie flying like a flag, had dived straight into the water. There was a great splash and he started striking out after the departing ship.

The crowd of onlookers gasped.

'Wow!' said one man. 'What's the matter with him?'

'Isn't that the man from The Grand?' said another.

'So it is,' said the first. 'Someone from the *Queen Canute* must have forgotten to pay for a cup of tea.'

The rest of the onlookers rolled their eyes, and tutted.

Meanwhile, Constable Brick was on his radio to the coastguard who had been waiting offshore for a signal from Operation Fish.

'Mayday, Mayday,' he said. 'It's Operation Fish. We have a swimmer!' And a moment later a cheer went up from the crowd as the rescue vessel came roaring towards Mr Harris and fished him out, dripping, into the boat.

The dogcatcher went bounding down the beach to meet them. 'Stand aside, there,' said the dogcatcher. 'I'm used to this sort of thing.' And he took off his shoes and socks and got ready with his net.

The residents were returning now, somewhat bemused.

'What's going on?' asked the Captain.

'I believe it's called "Operation Fish"', said Margot. 'But it's not going quite as planned.'

'Lord! Is that Kenneth?' cried Mrs Harris.

'Aye aye! Man overboard!' shouted the Captain. And he thundered down the ramp in his Wellington boots.

The dogcatcher had Mr Harris under the net now. He was wriggling like a fish and it was fortunate that the Captain was there to wade in and help pull him out of the water. Everyone watched as they dragged Mr Harris up on to the sand. Poor man – he had lost his glasses and his hair was plastered wetly to his head. The Captain and the dogcatcher each took an arm and marched him back up the ramp.

'Come on, Kenneth,' said Margot kindly, as they drew near. 'Let's get you out of your wet things.'

A bedraggled Mr Harris allowed himself to be helped down the hall supported by Nigel on one side and Mrs Harris on the other, his shoes squelching at every step. The rest of the residents followed them inside. The show was over now. The photographers snapped a few last pictures then slung their cameras over their shoulders and strolled off down the street. The reporters jumped into their cars, slammed the doors and drove off with a screech of wheels. The crowd began to disperse.

'I'm sorry, constable,' said Margot. 'I don't know what came over him.' She shook her head sadly. 'I blame myself. It's high time I took a more *active* role in the hotel. It's all been a little too much for Mr Harris.'

'Are you sure you can manage?' asked Constable Brick.

'Oh yes,' said Margot.

'Very good,' said the constable. 'If he causes any more trouble you'll let me know, won't you?'

'I certainly will.'

'It's good to see you up and about again,' said Constable Brick, tipping his hat before he too strode off down the street.

Chapter 19

Only Toby now remained at the end of the pier. He was leaning out over the railings with the wind rippling the thin cloth of his pyjamas. There went the last boat of the season; from now on the seaside town would be quiet. Cafés would close on Sundays and there would no longer be the big display of cakes at The Grand. There would be a chill in the air and the sky would turn wintery. The residents would bring the chairs inside again; they would light the fire in the bar and sit round and play card games. Cook would make potato and leek soup and treacle pudding and custard and they would have to turn the lights on earlier and earlier. It would be quiet this winter without the Flots. Toby sniffed sadly and folded his arms across his chest.

'Well – there they go,' said a voice behind him.

'Margot!'

Margot put her arm round Toby and together they watched the ship from the end of the pier.

'Do you think they'll come back?' said Toby.

'Of course they will.'

'But they might find somewhere they like better.'

'Without Cook's cream cakes?' said Margot. 'I doubt it.'

'Without Mr Harris,' said Toby.

Margot squeezed Toby against her. 'I don't think we need worry about Mr Harris any more,' she said. 'Nobody believes a word he says.'

'But – will you go back to bed again? Like

you did before?'

'I will not,' said Margot, most definitely. 'There's far too much to do.'

'To do?'

'To change,' said Margot darkly. 'Oh yes, there's a lot to change. She leaned on the railings and peered out to sea. Dark clouds were gathering over the horizon, and swathes of rain were drawing nearer. 'Toby,' she said, 'have you ever wondered where you came from?'

Toby followed Margot's gaze. 'Yes,' he said. 'Every time a ship comes in, I think that maybe there'll be someone aboard who didn't just come for tea and cakes, but who came back to get *me*.'

'Oh dear,' said Margot. 'If only I'd known earlier. I always suspected it, but I could never quite be sure . . .'

'Known what?'

Margot looked down kindly at Toby, 'I know who your parents are,' she said. 'The Flots told me.'

'Who? How do the Flots know?'

Margot sighed. 'I'd better start at the beginning,' she said. She took a deep breath. 'I was the one who left you on the bed in number twenty-three.'

'You! Are *you* my mother?'

'No, no,' said Margot, quickly. 'I found you on the beach.'

'The beach?'

'Yes. Sometimes I'd get up very early and put on my dressing gown and go down to the beach while no one was about. One morning I found you. It was a year after the Duke's ship went down.'

'I was just lying there?'

'You were wrapped in a blanket with *DD* embroidered on it. There was nobody about. What could I do? I brought you back inside. No one was awake. I was going to take you back to my room, but the door to room 23 was open, and the bed was made, so I decided to put you in there until everyone else woke up, and let them decide what to do with you. You were very good, you went right to sleep. I went back to bed.

Well! Next thing I knew it was midday and everyone was up and about, and the bed in room 23 was empty. I went downstairs and asked Mrs Harris where you'd gone. "Shhh!" she said. "We're not telling Kenneth or he'll make us send him to the orphanage. Cook has got him in the kitchen and she's giving him his bottle. Isn't it exciting! Who do you think has left him here?"

So you see, everyone wanted to take care of you, and you seemed happy enough. So I went back to bed. You have to remember, I wasn't really well. I didn't have the energy to care about anything, I just wanted to fester in bed all day.' She shook her head sadly. 'I thought they'd all take care of you,' she said. 'I had no idea how hard Mr Harris made you work . . .'

'But what about my parents?' cried Toby. 'Weren't they looking for me?'

Margot sighed. 'No,' she said sadly. 'They couldn't. Do you know what *DD* stands for?'

Toby reached in his pocket and brought out the Duke's ring. 'The Duke of Dudley?'

'Yes!' cried Margot. 'No one suspected it but me. You went down with the Duke's ship.'

Toby shook his head. 'I can't have done,' he said, confused. 'The ship went down a year before you found me – you said so yourself.'

'I know,' said Margot. 'But someone rescued you and looked after you for a whole year.'

'What? Who?'

Margot squeezed Toby's hand in hers. 'The Flots!' she said. 'They rescued you from the sinking ship, and they took you back to their cave, and they looked after you until you were starting to crawl. It was a wrench to let you go, Gaynor said, but it wasn't the life for a boy. You needed to be on dry land. They knew me because they'd seen me walking on the beach. They waited weeks, they said, for the right moment to leave you on the sand for me to find.'

Now it was all beginning to make sense to Toby. So that was why the Flots had been so pleased to see him, why they had been watching him so long! That was why the baby from the Duke's ship had never been found. That was why . . .

'So you mean my father . . . my mother . . .'

'Yes,' said Margot, nodding. 'Your parents were the Duke and Duchess of Dudley!'

There was a long silence, and Toby stared out to sea as though looking for the ship that would never come for him.

'The Flots wanted me to give you this,' said Margot. And she brought out a large rusty key from a pocket in her skirt.

'The Duke's jewels?' said Toby, taking the key.

'That's right,' said Margot. 'They're all yours. The Flots have been waiting until you were old enough to return them to you.'

Toby just stood there, staring at the key in his hand. Then he looked back out to sea. The little dark speck that had been the *Queen Canute* had disappeared beyond the horizon.

'Come on,' said Margot wrapping her arm

around his shoulders. 'Let's go inside.' And they made their way slowly back down the pier into the hotel, and shut the door behind them.

Outside the wind was getting up. The gulls lifted and tilted over the promenade and out over the ocean the clouds were gathering – great rotating columns of cloud, getting nearer all the time. Then the sky darkened, lights went on inside, and the wind flung the first few drops of rain against the windows of The Grand Hotel.

Margot *was true to her word: things have
certainly changed at The Grand. If you go
there now you'll hardly recognize the place.
Three diamond rings from Toby's inheritance
have restored the hotel to its former glory.
Gone are the threadbare carpets and the
chipped china. The chandelier sparkles and
there are lilies on the reception desk and
cakes every day.*

*Margot is about somewhere. You can hear
her singing. She's probably got her sleeves
rolled up, helping Cook in the kitchen. She
runs the place now. And look at Mr Harris!
He's playing poker with the residents – and*

*losing, by the look of it. But who's that
running down the pier at full tilt? Two boys
racing neck and neck, both laughing. Can
one of them be Nigel? I hardly recognize him,
laughing like that. And the tall, lanky boy in
a sailor suit, just pulling ahead – he's got bare
feet. Surely not! It can't be. It is! It's Toby. And
coming after them, running heavily in his
Wellington boots and his best blazer and
shouting 'Wait for me!' is the Captain. It looks
like they're going to meet a boat . . . and there
it is! It's in the distance, still – a tall white
cruise ship set in tiers like a wedding cake.
The first ship of the season.*